POINT GUARD PRANK

BY JAKE MADDOX

TEXT BY
THOMAS KINGSLEY TROUPE

ILLUSTRATIONS BY
SEAN TIFFANY

STONE ARCH BOOKS
a capstone imprint

Jake Maddox books are published by Stone Arch Books
A Capstone Imprint
1710 Roe Crest Drive
North Mankato, Minnesota 56003
www.capstonepub.com

Library of Congress Cataloging-in-Publication Data
Maddox, Jake.
  Point guard prank / by Jake Maddox; text by Thomas Kingsley Troupe;
illustrated by Sean Tiffany.
      p. cm. — (Jake Maddox sports story)
  Summary: Somebody is playing nasty tricks on Ryan DeMoss, point guard for
the Hillcrest Hammers, and it is starting to interfere with his game right before
the big tournament.
  ISBN 978-1-4342-4009-5 (library binding) — ISBN 978-1-4342-4207-5 (pbk.)
  1. Basketball stories. 2. Practical jokes—Juvenile fiction. 3. Tricks—Juvenile
fiction. 4. Friendship—Juvenile fiction. [1. Basketball—Fiction. 2. Practical jokes—
Fiction. 3. Tricks—Fiction. 4. Friendship—Fiction.] I. Troupe, Thomas Kingsley. II.
Tiffany, Sean, ill. III. Title.
  PZ7.M25643Poi 2012
  813.6—dc23   2011052568

Graphic Designer: Russell Griesmer
Production Specialist: Danielle Ceminsky

Photo Credits: Shutterstock 30941719 (Cover), Shutterstock 43565725 (p. 64, 70,
71, 72), Shutterstock/Nicemonkey 71713762 (p. 3)

Printed and bound in the USA.
010276R

TABLE OF CONTENTS

CHAPTER 1
PROBLEMS ON THE COURT

Point guard Ryan DeMoss dribbled the ball down the court as the rest of the Hillcrest Hammers got into position. They were down by three points in their game against the Westfield Rangers. There were less than two minutes left on the clock.

The Rangers were a tough team, and Ryan knew they weren't about to let up now. Not when the state tournament was just two wins away.

"Let's go, Hammers!" a fan shouted. Immediately, the rest of the Hillcrest basketball fans stomped their feet on the wooden bleachers. It sounded like thunder, and Ryan couldn't help but smile.

As Ryan crossed midcourt, he passed the ball to his teammate Josh. He watched as Josh dribbled to the left of the key and stopped, blocked by Rangers number 14. Josh jumped and faked a shot to the hoop. Then he pivoted on his right foot and fired a pass to Stefan. A quick Rangers defender snatched the ball and headed down court.

"Big defense, guys!" Ryan shouted as the Hammers raced to the other end of the court to defend their hoop. He stuck close to his guy, number 3. Ryan glanced at the clock. There were only ninety seconds left in the game.

Charlie moved in on the Rangers center and slapped at the ball, knocking it loose. The ball bounced twice, and Ryan was on it. He snatched it up and dribbled down the court. He heard the rest of the Rangers and his team running behind him as the crowd began to cheer.

This is it, Ryan thought. *An easy layup and we have a chance!*

Ryan dribbled past the free-throw line and moved to the right for his easy two-point shot. He brought the ball up. As he rose up on his left foot, he heard a loud, clanking noise from the crowd. It sounded like a cowbell.

Ryan's concentration was broken, and he fired the ball right into the underside of the hoop. The basketball bounced down and out of bounds.

What was that? Ryan wondered, looking into the crowd. The Hammer fans were shaking their heads and looking around, too.

Josh ran up to Ryan and clapped him on the back. "Shake it off," Josh said. "We still have time."

Ryan watched the Rangers throw the ball in from the end line. His team scrambled and chased the boys from Westfield down the court.

Number 14 broke away, turned, and fired a wild shot at the basket. It missed and dropped neatly into the hands of Stephen, the other point guard for the Hammers. He was quick with rebounds.

"Go, go!" Stephen shouted, and passed the ball.

Ryan ran back down the court and watched as one of his teammates got the ball, drove it down the middle of the key, and nailed a nice jump shot.

"You still in the game, Ry?" Josh asked as they got ready to defend their basket once more.

"Yeah," Ryan said. "I'm fine."

But he wasn't. The cowbell, or whatever he'd heard, still bothered him. It was almost as if someone had wanted him to miss. The only problem was that Ryan couldn't figure out who it could have been.

"Ryan! Get your head in the game!" Coach Nielsen shouted from the bench. Ryan turned just as a loose ball bounced past him. He moved to go after it, but was a second too late. Stefan ran past, snatched it up, and drove it to the basket.

The crowd began to count down the last few seconds of the game as Stefan took the shot. It dropped through the hoop right at the buzzer.

The Hammers had won, but just barely. Ryan didn't join his teammates as they cheered and celebrated. Instead, he looked out into the crowd of fans.

Someone's trying to make me screw up, he thought. *But why?*

CHAPTER 2
WHAT'S GOING ON?

In the locker room after the game, Ryan threw his towel at the lockers.

"What's wrong?" Josh asked. "You know we won, right?"

Ryan nodded. Then he sat down on the bench between the rows of lockers. He put his face in his hands and shook his head. After a deep breath, he looked up to face his team.

"Didn't you guys hear that cowbell just as I was going for the layup?" Ryan asked. "It totally threw me off! There's no way I should've missed that shot."

"It happens," Stefan said with a shrug. "I missed a free throw last week, and I never miss a free throw."

Ryan nodded. "It's not like I never miss a shot," he said. "But I think someone is messing with me."

"Well, maybe," Josh said. "Someone from the other team was probably trying to make you miss."

"But it came from the Hillcrest side," Ryan said. "I know it did."

"It was probably an accident," Brady said. "The cheerleaders hand those bells out for their big cheers. Maybe someone just moved his around at the wrong time."

Brady finished his bottle of water and tossed it in the recycling bin. "You don't really think someone is messing with you, do you?" he added. "Someone from our school?"

Ryan shrugged. "I don't know," he said. "But it's not the first time weird stuff like this has happened to me. Remember last week?"

Josh opened his locker. "Yeah," he said. "Someone put all of those thumbtacks on the bottom of your shoes. You almost wiped out when you put them on."

"Right," Ryan said. "I figured it was one of you guys, playing a joke. But after tonight, I don't think so anymore. Someone is out to get me."

"That doesn't make sense, though," Josh said.

"We're one game away from being in the big tournament," Brady added. "Why would anyone from Hillcrest do something like that? You'd think they'd want us to win."

"I don't know," Ryan replied. He grabbed his bag from his locker. "But it's got to stop. It's messing with my game."

CHAPTER 3
A NOTE FROM MOM

As Ryan left the locker room, Coach Nielsen called to him. "Hold up a second, Ryan," Coach said.

Oh great, Ryan thought. *Here's where Coach tells me I won't be starting next week because of how I played tonight.*

Coach Nielsen walked over to him, holding his clipboard. "Pretty good game tonight," Coach said. "You guys are playing well."

"Thanks," Ryan said. "The noise in the stands threw me off a bit, but otherwise —"

Coach interrupted him. "I got a note from your mom," he said.

"Really?" Ryan said. "What's it about?"

Coach lifted up his clipboard. "I've got it right here," he said. "Let me read it to you."

Ryan felt his face getting hot. *Why would my mom write a note to Coach Nielsen?* he wondered. It didn't seem like something she would do, not without telling him.

"'Dear Coach Nielsen, please excuse Ryan from practice all of next week,'" Coach read aloud. "'He is suffering from a sour stomach, and his doctor insists that he spend time in bed.'"

Coach Nielsen continued, "'I know the next game is a big one, but we must be careful with his health. Thank you for understanding. Fondly, Mrs. DeMoss.'"

Ryan was confused. "My stomach isn't sour," he said. "What does that even mean? And I haven't even been to the doctor for months. Where did you get that note?"

"It was on my desk," Coach said. "I found it there after the game." He held up the note. "Does this look like your mom's writing?"

Ryan looked at the paper. The handwriting was in cursive, and it was written in red pen.

"This isn't my mom's writing," Ryan said. "She writes in all capital letters. This looks like how a girl my age would write."

"I'll have to double-check with your folks to be sure," Coach said, taking the letter back. "But I have to admit, I was worried. We've got a giant game ahead of us and we need you, even if you do have a sour stomach."

"I don't have a sour stomach," Ryan said. "Seriously. I'm not sure where that came from. It's just plain weird."

"Good, good," Coach said. "Well, I'll see you next week. Great game tonight, pal."

"Okay," Ryan said. But he didn't really feel okay.

Seriously, he thought. *What is going on?*

CHAPTER 4
NOT AGAIN

All weekend, Ryan thought about his prank problem. He was sure someone was trying to make him look bad. But he tried hard to keep his mind on basketball when Monday rolled around.

After school, he and the rest of the Hillcrest Hammers headed for the locker room for basketball practice. Everything seemed normal.

But when he opened up his gym bag, his heart almost stopped. There, stuffed inside Ryan's gym bag, was something big, pink, and fluffy.

"What is this?" Ryan shouted.

The rest of his team gathered around to look.

"It's like what a ballerina wears," Danny said. "What do you call those things?"

Stefan nodded. "Tutus," he said. He blushed and added, "I have three sisters."

Ryan shook his head. "Seriously," he said. "What is going on here?"

"Maybe you grabbed the wrong bag from home," Josh suggested.

"No one in my family wears stuff like this," Ryan said.

Brady snapped his fingers and moved in closer. "I've got it," he said. "It's probably someone from Northfield. If we beat them, we're going to the state championship and they're not. Maybe they're trying to throw you off your game."

"Why would they just mess with *me*?" Ryan asked. "It's not like I'm the best player on the team. Why isn't anyone else getting pranked?"

The Hammers were silent. No one could explain why Ryan was being targeted.

"You know what the worst part is?" Ryan asked. "My practice gear is gone. Replaced with this . . ."

"Tutu," Stefan said again.

"Right," Ryan said.

Ryan reached deeper into the bag and pulled out two pink shoes with long ribbons attached to them. "Where are my sneakers?" he asked. "And what are these weird shoes?"

"Ballet slippers," Stefan said.

"Wow," Charlie said. "Someone *really* doesn't want you to practice."

Just then, the locker room door crashed open. Heavy footsteps approached.

"What's the hold up in here, boys?" Coach Nielsen shouted.

Great, Ryan thought. *After the fake sour stomach note last week, this is just what I need.* He quickly stuffed the tutu and shoes back into his bag, but it was too late. Coach came around the corner and saw them all, still in their school clothes, standing around Ryan's gym bag. A fluffy burst of pink stuck out from the zippered opening.

"Come with me, Mr. DeMoss," Coach said, pointing at Ryan. "Let's have a talk. The rest of you, get changed and hit the court!"

CHAPTER 5
COACH'S ADVICE

"Close the door behind you," Coach said. "And have a seat."

Ryan sat down in Coach Nielsen's small, cramped office. "So, what's going on, Ryan?" Coach asked.

"I don't know, Coach," Ryan began. "But I think someone wants to make me look like a horrible basketball player."

"What makes you think that?" asked Coach.

"A lot of things," said Ryan. "A couple of weeks ago, someone put thumbtacks on the bottom of my shoes. Then last week at the game, someone rang a cowbell right when I was about to shoot. It almost cost us the game."

"Anything else?" asked Coach.

"Oh, yeah," said Ryan. "There was that fake note about me having to miss practice. And now today, there was a tutu and ballet shoes in my bag."

"The game of basketball is a head game, son," Coach Nielsen said. "No matter what happens outside the court, you need to keep your head in the game. There could be elephants doing backflips and a fireworks show above the bleachers. I don't care. Keep your focus. Do you understand?"

Ryan sighed and nodded.

"There are always going to be distractions," Coach said. "But the really good players don't even notice that kind of thing. You can have jokers in the stands waving flags as you're trying to sink a free throw."

"Like in pro games," Ryan said.

"That's right," Coach said. "But if you shut all of that stuff court out, it's like they're not even there."

"Okay," Ryan said. "I just need to focus."

"That's my advice," Coach said. "Simple."

"Thanks," Ryan said. "But what about the stuff outside the games? Like the tutu."

Coach Nielsen shook his head. "That I can't help you with," Coach said. "I mean, are you sure it was your bag?"

Ryan nodded. "It was someone's idea of a prank," he said. "Only I'm not laughing. Not at all."

Coach Nielsen shrugged. "I'll help you find some practice gear," he said. "Get your head back in the game. We've got a state championship to win."

CHAPTER 6
A STINKY TRICK

Coach Nielsen found Ryan some old shorts, a faded T-shirt, and a pair of high-tops that creaked with every step. Practice was horrible. Ryan couldn't concentrate. He missed shots he always sank and played defense like he was half asleep. The pranks were all he could think about.

When practice was over, Ryan headed out with the rest of the guys, talking about the big game against Northfield on Saturday. But then he realized he'd left his backpack in the locker room.

"I'll see you tomorrow, guys," he said. "I forgot my bag."

Ryan headed back toward the gym. Along the way, he stopped at the giant trophy case outside the main office. It was loaded with trophies from past basketball, football, gymnastics, and swimming teams.

Ryan really wanted his team to bring a trophy home for the case. It had been too long since the Hillcrest Hammers had taken first place in the state championships.

As Ryan entered the empty gymnasium, a nearby door squeaked and clicked closed. He stood for a moment and listened.

"Coach?" Ryan called. His voice echoed a bit within the big space.

There was no answer.

Ryan headed to the locker room, his gym bag slung over his shoulder. As he entered, he heard footsteps.

Someone else is in here! Ryan thought. His eyes widened. *Maybe it's whoever's been doing all the pranks.*

Being as quiet as he possible, Ryan pressed himself against a set of lockers and slowly slid toward the end. He peeked his head around the corner. There, squatting down in front of his gym locker, was a boy in a black sweatshirt and a pair of faded jeans.

He's messing with my locker! Ryan realized. Suddenly he was too angry to be sneaky anymore. He stepped out from the wall.

"Hey!" Ryan shouted. "What are you doing to my locker?"

Surprised, the boy banged his head against the metal locker as he stood up. "Ow," he groaned, holding his head. Then he faced Ryan.

It was Ryan's classmate Ned. They had history and English together.

"Ned?" Ryan said. "What are you doing?

Ned fumbled the little packet he was holding. Green powder spilled out, coating his sweatshirt.

"Oh, great," Ned cried, looking down at his shirt. "This is just great."

And that was when the stink hit.

CHAPTER 7
SOUR GRAPES

"Ugh," Ryan said. "What is that smell?"

Ned plugged his nose. "It's stink powder!" he said.

Ryan covered his mouth and his nose. The powder smelled like wet garbage left to rot in the sun. It made his eyes water and left a bad taste in his mouth. And the stink powder was all over Ned's sweatshirt.

"Take off your shirt!" Ryan shouted. "Throw it in the showers or something!"

Ned nodded, coughing. He peeled his sweatshirt off and ran toward the showers. He threw the shirt down on the wet, tiled floor. Ryan followed. He kicked the shirt under one of the showerheads. With a twist, he turned the shower on full blast and soaked the shirt with hot water.

They ran back to Ryan's locker. "Wow," Ryan said. "That was bad."

"Yeah," Ned agreed.

"So," Ryan said. "You're the one that's been messing with me."

Ned shook his head. "I haven't been messing with you," he said. "I don't even know what you're talking about."

"What?" Ryan said, frowning. "I caught you messing with my locker!"

"Okay, okay," Ned said. "It was me."

"Why?" Ryan asked. "What did I ever do to you?"

Ned sat down on the end of a bench between the lockers. "Remember tryouts for the basketball team?" he asked. "A few months ago?"

Ryan nodded. He knew that Ned had tried out, but he hadn't made the team. "What does that have to do with me?" Ryan asked.

"I found out that the last spot on the team was between you and me," Ned said. "Coach had already picked everyone else. He just wasn't sure about who he wanted as the second point guard."

"How do you know that?" Ryan asked.

I can't believe I was the last guy picked, he thought. He wished Ned hadn't told him.

"My dad is friends with Coach Nielsen," Ned admitted. "Dad probably thought it would make me feel better to know I almost made the team."

"That doesn't make sense," Ryan said, shaking his head. "Why are you mad at me? For making the team? All I did was try out, like you did. You should be mad at Coach Nielsen!"

"You're right," Ned said. "Maybe I should put some stink powder in his office."

"Not a good idea," Ryan said. "Give the stink powder a rest."

"You're probably right," Ned said. "I just got so mad. And now that you guys might end up in the big tournament, I feel even worse about not being on the team."

Ryan sat down next to Ned. "Look, I'm sorry you didn't make the team," Ryan said. "It was probably hard for Coach to have to choose between us."

"Maybe," Ned said. "But when I didn't make the cut, I just didn't know what else to do. I wanted you off the team. I'm sorry."

"Well, do me a favor," Ryan said. "Don't mess with my stuff anymore, okay?"

"Okay," Ned said. "Sorry. It wasn't cool of me to do that."

Ryan got up and went into the shower to turn the water off. He twisted the water out of the soaking wet sweatshirt and returned, tossing the shirt to Ned.

"Thanks," Ned said.

"No problem," Ryan replied. "You think maybe I can get my practice stuff back?"

"Yeah," Ned said and smiled. "Any chance you still have that tutu? I'll never hear the end of it if my sister doesn't get it back."

CHAPTER 8
ONE-ON-ONE

After Ryan exchanged the tutu and ballet slippers for his practice clothes, he and Ned walked out of the gym and down the hall together. Ned stopped at his locker and pulled out a basketball. "You up for a little one-on-one?" he asked, smiling.

"Not here," Ryan said, shaking his head. "How about at the park?"

"You're on," Ned replied.

Ryan and Ned headed to a nearby park. There, they found an old basketball hoop that was missing its net. Though he was tired from practice and hungry for dinner, Ryan was excited to play. It had been forever since he'd played just for fun.

"We'll play to eleven points," Ned said. "Then I need to get home and eat."

"And take a shower," Ryan said. "I can still smell that stink powder."

Ned grinned. "Your ball," he said.

Ryan drove to the basket and was surprised that Ned stuck right to him. Ned's defense was tough to drive through. When Ryan turned, Ned was there. When Ryan faked by pretending to shoot at the basket, Ned didn't take the bait. They traded points, one after the other. Ryan had to work hard for every shot he made.

Ned pulled off some fancy footwork and even spun around, all while dribbling. It was a flashy move that Ryan wasn't ready for. He found himself laughing as Ned sank the shot.

"Nice," Ryan said, clapping. "Where did you learn to show off like that?"

"Not sure," Ned said, smiling. "Maybe I scared Coach Nielsen when he was picking the team. Most coaches don't want their players showing off."

"Maybe," Ryan said. "But you're good. I think you're probably better than half of the guys on the Hammers."

Ned grinned and said, "You don't need to say that to make me feel better."

"Seriously," Ryan said. "You play like this for tryouts next season and you'll definitely make the team."

"Thanks," Ned said. Then he tossed the basketball to Ryan and added, "Your ball."

* * *

One game turned into two, and two games turned into four. Ryan could hardly believe it when he realized how late it was.

"Oh, wow," Ryan said. "I need to get home."

"Last point of the game," Ned said and drove to the basket.

"Not so fast!" Ryan shouted. He'd learned quickly to watch Ned's midsection to play tighter defense. If Ned shifted right, he stepped right with him. So when Ned stopped with his back to the basket, Ryan knew he had him.

"Game over," Ryan said, slapping at the ball.

Just then, Ned jumped and turned around in midair. He sailed the ball in a high arc and shot it. It passed cleanly through the bent park hoop and bounced once before hitting the grass.

"Nothing but net," Ned said. "Well, if there was one."

CHAPTER 9
GAME ON

The rest of the week flew by, and before Ryan knew it, Saturday's big game against the Northfield Vipers was about to start. He and the rest of the Hillcrest Hammers gathered around the bench. Coach Nielsen squatted down in the middle of the group of boys and gave a quick pep talk.

"Watch your zones, keep your heads in the game, and we'll take this one," Coach said. "Simple."

Ryan shouted "Hammers!" with the rest of the team. After figuring out that Ned had been the one doing all the pranks, Ryan felt confident and ready to play.

We're taking this one, Ryan thought. *Game time!*

As Ryan headed out to center court with Josh, he looked out into the packed stands. It was easy to find the Hillcrest fans. Almost an entire side of the court was decked out in blue and white.

"Are you ready for this, Ryan?" asked Josh. "This is our ticket to the big game!"

"Oh, I'm ready," Ryan said. He gave Josh a high-five. "These guys won't even know what hit 'em."

Ryan and Josh took their positions in center court for the jump.

The Hillcrest Hammers got the ball and immediately drove it down the court. Charlie bounced it to Ryan. He quickly shot and sank the first basket of the game.

"Nice!" Stefan shouted as they ran to the other end of the court together. "You're back!"

Ryan smiled and watched as the Vipers threw the ball in from the sidelines.

It feels good to be back, Ryan thought. Even so, he knew he had to keep his focus and work hard. The Vipers weren't going to just let them win.

The Vipers moved in on the Hammer defense. Ryan closely guarded his guy, number 13. The Vipers player couldn't get close to the basket, and he finally passed the ball away.

As the ball left number 13's fingers, Ryan swatted it down, grabbed it, and fired it over to Josh. Quickly, Josh broke away and made an easy layup. Within a matter of seconds, the Hammers were ahead by four.

Ryan played better than he had all year. He was leading the team in rebounds, and he found himself in scoring position more than usual.

The rest of the Hammers seemed to have an extra spark, too. Stefan made three incredible baskets in a row, and whenever the ball was stolen, Josh was ready to take it in for a layup. By halftime, the Hammers led 28 to 21.

"Looking good, boys," Coach Nielsen said as his players jogged to the bench. "Keep up the tight defense, and we'll walk away with a win!"

Ryan smiled. He grabbed a bottle of water and squirted some into his mouth. *This could be the year of the Hammers,* he thought.

"Let's go, boys," Coach shouted at the buzzer. "Keep doing what you're doing. Let's take it to 'em and lock in the big game!"

The team huddled up and put their hands in. "Go Hammers!" they all shouted.

Heading into the second half, the excitement of playing in the semifinals continued to build. It seemed like Charlie couldn't miss, and he racked up nearly twenty points. Meanwhile, the rest of the team ran like a well-tuned machine.

"Keep your head in the game, guys," Coach shouted from the bench. "It isn't over yet!"

Ryan looked up at the scoreboard. It was 57 to 43, with just under five minutes left on the clock. The Hammers had a big lead, but a lot could happen in the last few minutes.

The Vipers' star player, number 42, dribbled around the Hammers' zone defense. He drove it down the middle and came face to face with Ryan.

Number 42 moved and Ryan was all over him with his hands up to make a shot impossible. Finally, 42 passed the ball away and Stefan stole it.

Ryan sprinted down the court. When Stefan got trapped by two Vipers players, he bounced the ball to Ryan. With a few seconds on the clock, Ryan sank another two-point basket.

As he ran to the other side of the court, Ryan saw his parents in the crowd, clapping and cheering. A few rows behind them, Ned whistled louder than anyone. Ryan smiled as the buzzer sounded.

The Hammers had won! They were headed for the state championship!

CHAPTER 10
PUNK BACK

"Got time for one a quick game?" Ryan asked as he and Ned walked near the beat-up court in the park a week later.

"Just one," Ned said. "I've got a game in about a half hour."

Ryan nodded. Ned had told him that he joined a local team that played every Saturday morning.

"You should play with us, Mr. State Championship," Ned said as Ryan bounced the ball to him. "Unless you're too much of a big shot."

Ryan shrugged. "Don't jinx us. We haven't won yet," he said. The big game was that night. "But maybe I *will* join your team," he added. "It would be good practice for next year."

"You're going to need all the practice you can get," said Ned. "You'll be facing me in tryouts."

Ryan grinned. "Come on. Let's play," he said.

"Game on," Ned said. He dribbled the ball and forced his way to the basket. He went up for a layup. The ball rolled across the open hoop and dropped to the other side.

"Whoa," Ned shouted. "How did . . ."

Ryan wasted no time. He scooped up the ball and made an easy layup in his basket.

"Did you see that?" Ned asked. He pointed back at the basket, puzzled. "I never miss those."

"There's a first time for everything, Ned," Ryan said. "It's 1 to 0. Your ball."

Ryan bounced the ball to his friend. Ned dribbled toward the basket, keeping Ryan away. He turned and fired his jump shot. The ball arced, struck the middle of the hoop, and bounced right out.

"That was perfect!" Ned shouted. "What's going on?"

Ryan laughed as the ball rolled out of bounds. He dropped to his knees and lay down. His sides hurt from laughing so hard.

"What's so funny?" Ned asked, confused. A hurt look crossed his face.

"Take another shot," Ryan said, still laughing.

Ned scooped up the ball and stood in front of the basket. He shot a perfect free throw. Then he watched as the ball bounced out from the middle of the hoop and back onto the court.

"No way," Ned said and started laughing. "What did you do?"

Ryan pointed to the basket. There was a layer of thick, shiny plastic wrap covering the hoop.

"I thought it was time to prank you back, buddy," Ryan said.

"You got me," Ned said, laughing. "You got me good."

ABOUT THE AUTHOR

Thomas Kingsley Troupe writes, makes movies, and works as a firefighter/EMT. He's written many books for kids, including *Legend of the Vampire* and *Mountain Bike Hero*, and has two boys of his own. He likes zombies, bacon, orange Popsicles, and reading stories to his kids. Thomas currently lives in Woodbury, Minnesota, with his super cool family.

ABOUT THE ILLUSTRATOR

When Sean Tiffany was growing up, he lived on a small island off the coast of Maine. Every day, from sixth grade until he graduated from high school, he had to take a boat to get to school. When Sean isn't working on his art, he works on a multimedia project called "OilCan Drive," which combines music and art. He has a pet cactus named Jim.

GLOSSARY

concentration (KON-suhn-tray-shuhn)—focused thoughts and attention

confident (KON-fuh-duhnt)—having a strong belief in your own abilities

distractions (diss-TRAC-shuhnz)—things that interrupt you or weaken your focus on what you are doing

free throw (FREE THROH)—a basketball shot worth one point that must be made from behind a specfic line and is given because of a foul by an opponent

jump shot (JUHMP SHOT)—a basketball shot made while jumping

layup (LAY-uhp)—a shot in basketball made from near the basket usually by playing the ball off the backboard

rebounds (REE-boundz)—acts of gaining possession of the ball after it has bounced off the backboard in a missed shot

DISCUSSION QUESTIONS

1. Ryan could not ignore the distractions on the court. If you were Ryan, would you be able to block out extra noises and other distractions while playing? If so, how?

2. Do you think that Coach Nielsen handled Ryan's concerns well? What would you have said if you were the coach?

3. Ned was disappointed that he didn't make the team. Think of a time that you were disappointed. How did you handle your disappointment?

WRITING PROMPTS

1. Write a scene that shows Ned actually doing one of his pranks. For example, you could show how he switched the clothes in the gym bag.

2. Have you ever pulled a prank on someone? Write about it.

3. Chapter 6 is told from Ryan's point of view. Now rewrite part of it from Ned's point of view.

The point guard leads a basketball team's offense. He controls the ball and delivers it to the right players as needed. The National Basketball Association (NBA) has seen its share of great point guards. Here are a few that rise above the rest.

→ JOHN STOCKTON

John Stockton played his entire nineteen-year career with the Utah Jazz. He holds the all-time record for assists (15,806) and steals (3,265). Though he is considered one of the greatest players of all time, he never won an NBA championship.

→ BOB COUSY

Nicknamed the Houdini of the Hardwood, Bob Cousy won six NBA championships with the Boston Celtics. He was named the NBA's most valuable player in 1957. Fans loved his fancy ball handling and no-look passes.

→ ISAIAH THOMAS

This Detroit Piston averaged 9.3 assists per game. The two-time NBA champ was also known for his shooting, especially at the end of close games. In a 1984 playoff game against the Knicks, Thomas scored 16 points in the final 91 seconds, forcing the game into overtime.

→ OSCAR ROBERTSON

An excellent all-around player, Cincinnati Royal Oscar Robertson scored an average of 30.8 points, 11.4 assists, and 12.5 rebounds per game in 1962. These stats made him the last player to average a triple double in a season.

→ IRVIN "MAGIC" JOHNSON

Often called the best point guard of all time, Magic Johnson led the Los Angeles Lakers to five championships. He's a three-time NBA MVP and a three-time Finals MVP. He also holds twelve different playoff records.

3 MORE GREAT BOOKS

FROM
JAKE MADDOX